For Reg and Muriel ~ E B

Here's hoping we all find our own pot of gold ~ C P

LITTLE TIGER PRESS

An imprint of Magi Publications

1 The Coda Centre, 189 Munster Road, London SW6 6AW

www.littletigerpress.com

First published in Great Britain 2008

A CIP catalogue record for this book is available from the British Library

Printed in China

10 9 8 7 6 5 4 3 2

Little Pip and the Rainbow Wish

Elizabeth Baguley   Caroline Pedler

LITTLE TIGER PRESS
London

Hidden away, small and wet, Pip huddled
beneath a hedge. While out in the open,
Milly and Spike played dodge-the-raindrop
and puddle-sploshing.

Pip wanted to join in, but he was such
a shy little mouse that he couldn't think
of a way to ask.

Pip watched as Spike
gave Milly a dandelion clock.
Together they wiggled and
whooped around it. Perhaps,
Pip thought, if I had
something to give them,
they would play with *me*.
He looked around him but
could see only scratchy
stones and patchy sky.

Just at that moment . . .

. . . a shining rainbow lit up the clouds. What a present *that* would be for Milly and Spike! They could slide down it, balance on it, make a tent under its colours. And he would be their friend.

But the rainbow was so far away . . .

. . . too high to reach on
the tips of his paws . . .

too far away to catch
with a bendy stick . . .

and his bounce was
just not bouncy enough.

No matter what he tried,
the rainbow was very, very up
and Pip was very, very down.

"What are you doing?" asked Milly,
who had stopped playing to watch.

Pip's tail blushed to its very tip.
"I wanted to catch the . . . er . . . er . . ."
"The rainbow?" said Spike. "That's
brilliant! We'll help!"

Spike clambered onto Milly's shoulders. "Come on, Pip," he called. "We need you, too." And he swung Pip right to the top of the mouse-tower.

The tower was sky-high. But then Pip began to wobble . . . the tower began to sway . . .

And
they
all
fell
into
a
jumbly
mouse
heap!

"We could just *wish* for
the rainbow," Pip said,
quietly.

"Good idea!" said Spike,
and together they squeezed
their wish into the sky.

But the rainbow stayed
just where it was.

Then Milly picked up the dandelion
clock. "Someone could fly to the rainbow!"
she said. "Who's lightest?"

"Me, me!" cried Pip, suddenly not shy at all.

Milly and Spike pulled Pip along, until the
wind scooped him up so high that he could
almost touch the rainbow.

He reached out his
paws. But the seeds
began to fall from the
dandelion clock, one . . .

by one . . .

by one.

And

Pip

sank

s l o w l y

back

to

earth.

"I didn't catch the rainbow," said Pip, sadly.

"You were very brave," said Milly, hugging him.

"We'll just have to think of another way," said Spike.

But at that very moment, the rain dripped to

a stop and the rainbow melted away and was gone.

"Don't go!" begged Pip. "Please don't go!"

"Don't worry," said Spike. "There'll be another rainbow."

"But I needed it," sniffed Pip. "To give to you and Milly, so that you would be my friends."

"But we *are* your friends!" said Milly.

"Who needs presents anyway?" said Spike.

Then off they raced, all together,
hopping and sploshing from puddle
to puddle, until the night sky burst
into a brilliant sparkling of stars.